A NOTE TO PARENTS

Reading Aloud with Your Child

Research shows that reading books aloud is the single most valuable support parents can provide in helping children learn to read.

- Be a ham! The more enthusiasm you display, the more your child will enjoy the book.
- Run your finger underneath the words as you read to signal that the print carries the story.
- Leave time for examining the illustrations more closely; encourage your child to find things in the pictures.
- Invite your youngster to join in whenever there's a repeated phrase in the text.
- Link up events in the book with similar events in your child's life.
- If your child asks a question, stop and answer it. The book can be a means to learning more about your child's thoughts.

Listening to Your Child Read Aloud

The support of your attention and praise is absolutely crucial to your child's continuing efforts to learn to read.

- If your child is learning to read and asks for a word, give it immediately so that the meaning of the story is not interrupted. DO NOT ask your child to sound out the word.
- On the other hand, if your child initiates the act of sounding out, don't intervene.
- If your child is reading along and makes what is called a miscue, listen for the sense of the miscue. If the word "road" is substituted for the word "street," for instance, no meaning is lost. Don't stop the reading for a correction.
- If the miscue makes no sense (for example, "horse" for "house"), ask your child to reread the sentence because you're not sure you understand what's just been read.
- Above all else, enjoy your child's growing command of print and make sure you give lots of praise. *You are your child's first teacher—and the most important one. Praise from you is critical for further risk-taking and learning.*

—Priscilla Lynch
Ph.D., New York University
Educational Consultant

Text copyright © 1993 by Judith Bauer Stamper.
Illustrations copyright © 1993 by Timothy Raglin.
CARTWHEEL BOOKS is a registered trademark of Scholastic Inc.
HELLO READER! is a registered trademark of Scholastic Inc.
All rights reserved. Published by Scholastic Inc.

Library of Congress Cataloging-in-Publication Data
Stamper, Judith Bauer.
Five funny frights / by Judith Bauer Stamper : illustrated by Tim Raglin.
p.   cm. — (Hello reader! Level 4)
Summary: A collection of five easy-to-read scary stories with humorous endings, including "The Skeleton," "The Scream," and "Bloody Fingers."
ISBN 0-590-46416-7
1. Horror tales, American.   2. Children's stories, American.
[1. Horror stories.   2. Humorous stories.   3. Short stories.]
I. Raglin, Tim. ill.   II. Title.   III. Title: 5 funny frights.
IV. Series.
PZ7.S78612F1   1993   92-44538
[E]—dc20   CIP   AC
12   11   10   9   8   7   6   5   4   3   2   1   3   4   5   6   7   8/9

Printed in the U.S.A.   23
First Scholastic printing, September 1993

FIVE
FUNNY
FRIGHTS

by Judith Bauer Stamper
Illustrated by Tim Raglin

Hello Reader!—Level 4

SCHOLASTIC INC.

New York   Toronto   London   Auckland   Sydney

THE SKELETON

It was the scariest night
of the year.
Ben was waiting for his friend.
Where could he be?
Ben started to shiver.

A bat swooped down from a tree
right over Ben's head.
Ben almost jumped out of his skin.
Then he started to run.

Ben ran and ran until he couldn't
run anymore.
Finally, he stopped and sat down on
a cold, hard rock to rest.
Just then, the moon came out and lit
up the sky.

Ben looked down at the rock he was
sitting on.
It wasn't a rock at all.
It was a tombstone!
Ben looked around him.
He was sitting in the middle of
a cemetery!

From close behind him, Ben heard
a noise.
He turned around and saw a
skeleton.
It was coming right at him!
Ben jumped up and started to run for
his life.

He ran faster than he had ever
run before.
But the skeleton chased right
after him.
It was getting closer and closer.

Ben turned his head to look
behind him.
The skeleton was only a few
feet away.
It had a gruesome grin on its face.
Then it reached out a bony hand to
grab Ben.
But it just missed him!

By now, Ben was only one block
from his house.
He tried to run faster, but his legs felt
like jelly.
All of a sudden, he tripped on a tree
root and fell down to the ground.

Ben scrambled back to his feet as
fast as he could.
But the skeleton was right in front
of him.
Ben looked into his grinning face.
And he screamed!

Then the skeleton reached out a
bony hand.
It tapped Ben on the shoulder
And it said . . .

"TAG, YOU'RE IT!"

THE SCREAM

Jenny was staying with her
grandmother.
Her grandmother lived in a big old
house that had twenty-two rooms.
And people said it was full of ghosts.

One night, Jenny couldn't go
to sleep.
She tossed and turned and tossed
and turned in her bed.
She was thinking about the stories.
Did ghosts really live in
her grandmother's house?

Then, outside her door, Jenny heard
a strange noise in the hallway.
She pricked up her ears.
The noise sounded like soft
footsteps.
They were going
down the stairs.

Jenny became more and more curious.

Slowly, she crept out of bed.

She opened the door to her room.

She started to follow the footsteps down the stairs.

Finally, Jenny reached the bottom of the stairs.

She heard a soft moan come from down the hallway.

She tiptoed toward it in the dark.

The moaning sound moved toward the front door.

Then Jenny heard the door creak open.

She crept through the dark toward
the door.
Then she stepped out onto the big
porch in front of the house.
Another moan floated through
the air.
Jenny could tell it was from the steps
leading into the garden.
Slowly, she tiptoed down the steps.

For a minute, the moaning sound
stopped.
Jenny heard nothing but the sound
of the crickets in the night.
Then, from out in the garden,
the moaning started again.
Jenny stepped toward it over
the cold, soft ground.

Suddenly she screamed,
"AAAAAAAAAAAAAAAAAH!"

Well, you'd scream, too,
IF YOU STUBBED YOUR TOE ON
A ROCK!

A DARK, DARK STORY

In a dark, dark wood,
there was a dark, dark house.

And in that dark, dark house,
there was a dark, dark hall.
And in that dark, dark hall,
there was a dark, dark stairway.

And up that dark, dark stairway,
there was a dark, dark attic.

And in that dark, dark attic,
there was a dark, dark trunk.
And in that dark, dark trunk,
there was a dark, dark coat.

And in that dark, dark coat,
there was a dark, dark pocket.
And in that dark, dark pocket,
there was a dark, dark box.
And in that dark, dark box,
there was . . .

A PINK JELLYBEAN!

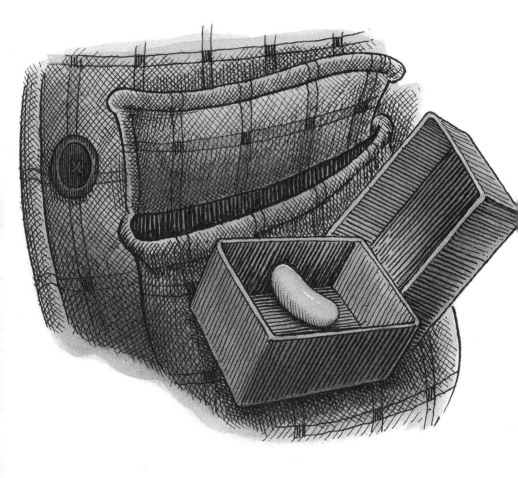

BLOODY FINGERS

Two brothers were camping out in
the woods.
They had gone on a long walk
through the tall, dark trees.
Now, they were lost.
The sun was sinking lower and lower
in the sky.

"I think camp is that way," one said.
"I think it's the other way," the
second said.
They stood looking at each other,
not knowing what to do.
Both of them were really scared.

Just then, they heard a sound behind
them.
Something was coming toward them
through the woods.
They turned around and looked.

It was a man, coming closer
and closer.
He was holding his hands up
in the air.
"Bloody fingers!" he called out
in a scary voice.

The two brothers looked at each
other with wide eyes.
Then they started to run.
The man ran after them.
"Bloody fingers!" he screamed.

The brothers ran faster and faster.
But the man kept up with them.
He held out his fingers.
They could see the blood!

"Bloody fingers!" the man kept
calling.
The boys were shaking with
fear now.
Then they saw their camp.
Maybe they could make it
to their tent!

The boys ran into the campground.
But the man kept right on running
after them.
"Bloody fingers!" he yelled.
He was getting closer and closer.

Just in time, the brothers ran into
their tent and hid under their cots.
Their mother and father were gone.
But their little sister was there.
Outside the tent, the man was still
screaming, "Bloody fingers!"

The little sister looked at her brothers
hiding under the cots.
Then she peeked through the tent
flap to look at the man.
"Bloody fingers!" he screamed
at her.

The girl picked up something from
a box in the tent.
Then she walked outside.
The man pointed his bloody fingers
at her.

"Bloody fingers!" he yelled.
"HAVE A BAND-AID!" she said.

GHOSTS!

One dark night, a boy was walking
home all alone.
Something about this night
made him feel afraid.

Suddenly rain came down in heavy
sheets.
The boy started to run.
He was still a long way from home.
And he had to find a dry place.

He ran down the road past an old
graveyard.
He looked over his shoulder at the
white tombstones, and ran even faster!
A short distance ahead was a big
barn in the middle of a field.
The barn looked old, but it would be
dry.

He pulled open the old barn door
and hurried inside.
He stood there, shivering.
The barn was dark but the boy found
a bale of hay and sat down on it.

A flash of lightning shot through the
sky.
For a second, it lit up the old barn.
The boy stared around him in shock.
Strange white shapes surrounded
him.

The boy screamed!
The ghosts must have followed him
from the graveyard!

Another flash of lightning lit the
barn.
The white shapes had moved closer
to him.
He jumped up from the bale of hay
and ran for the barn door.
But he tripped over one of the
ghosts!
"BAA-A-A!" it said.

The lightning flashed again.
The boy saw the white shapes clearly
for the first time.